W9-BNA-314

THE GIRL WHO LOVED WILD HORSES

Also by the author:

BUFFALO WOMAN

DEATH OF THE IRON HORSE

THE GIFT OF THE SACRED DOG

THE GREAT RACE

STAR BOY

THE GIRL WHO LOVED WILD HORSES

Story and Illustrations by PAUL GOBLE

BRADBURY PRESS
NEW YORK

The text of this book is set in 12 pt. Century Schoolbook. The illustrations are full-color pen-and-ink and watercolor paintings, the black line separated by the artist from the base plates, reproduced in combined line and halftone.
Library of Congress cataloging in Publication Data
Goble, Paul. The Girl Who Loved Wild Horses.
Summary: Though she is fond of her people, a girl prefers to live among the wild horses where she is truly happy and free.
[1. Fairy tales. 2. Indians of North America—Fiction. 3. Horses—Fiction] I. Title.
PZ8.G537Gi [E] 77-20500 ISBN 0-02-736570-0

Bradbury Press, An Affiliate of Macmillan, Inc., 866 Third Avenue, New York, NY 10022, Collier Macmillan Canada, Inc.
Manufactured in the United States of America. First Edition

15 14 13 12 11 10 9 8

For Bonnie
who loves horses
and
for Janet

The people were always moving from place to place following the herds of buffalo. They had many horses to carry the tipis and all their belongings. They trained their fastest horses to hunt the buffalo.

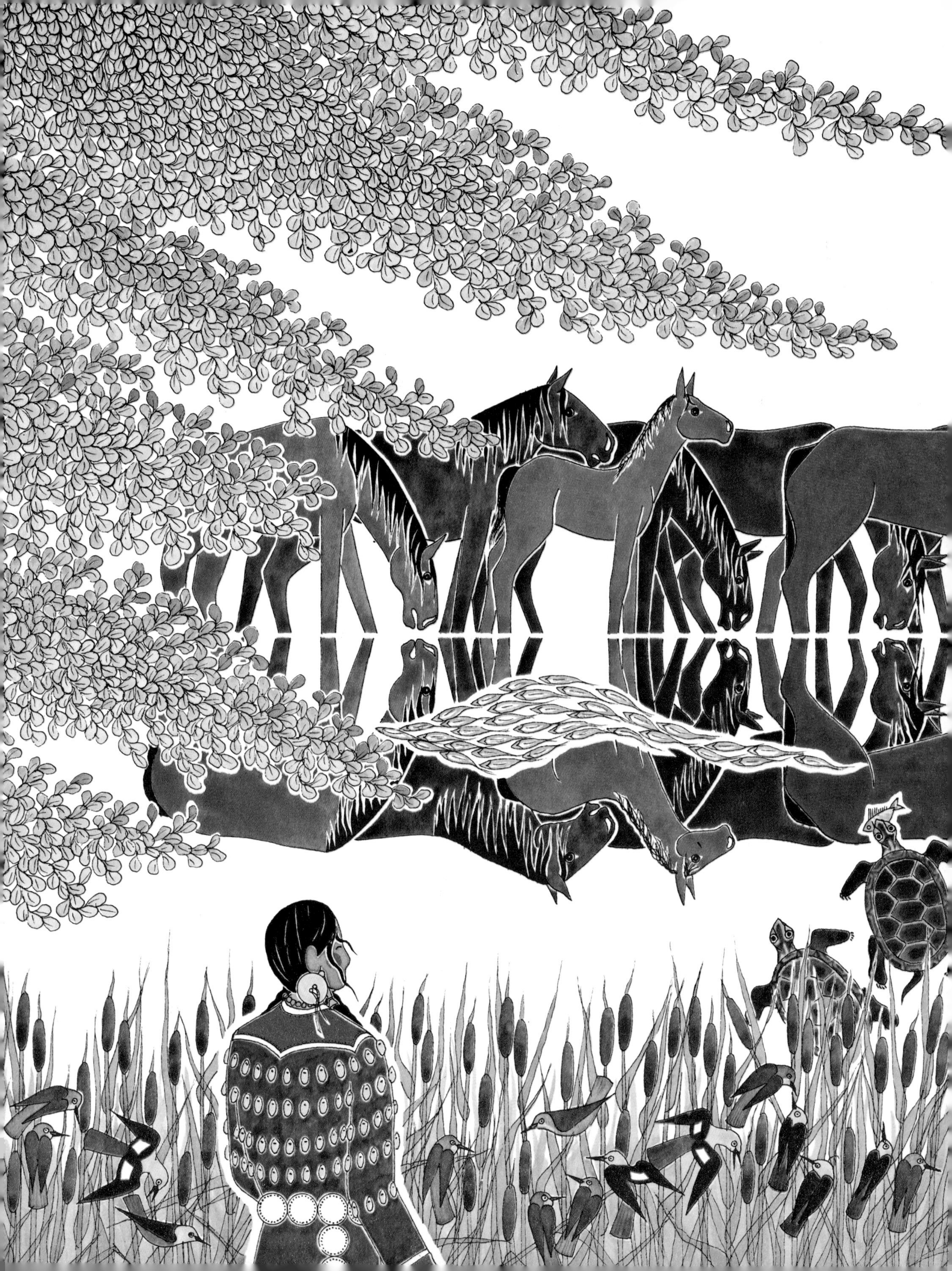

There was a girl in the village who loved horses. She would often get up at daybreak when the birds were singing about the rising sun. She led the horses to drink at the river. She spoke softly and they followed.

People noticed that she understood horses in a special way. She knew which grass they liked best and where to find them shelter from the winter blizzards. If a horse was hurt she looked after it.

Every day when she had helped her mother carry water and collect firewood, she would run off to be with the horses. She stayed with them in the meadows, but was careful never to go beyond sight of home.

One hot day when the sun was overhead she felt sleepy. She spread her blanket and lay down. It was nice to hear the horses eating and moving slowly among the flowers. Soon she fell asleep.

A faint rumble of distant thunder did not waken her. Angry clouds began to roll out across the sky with lightning flashing in the darkness beneath. But the fresh breeze and scent of rain made her sleep soundly.

Suddenly there was a flash of lightning, a crash and rumbling which shook the earth. The girl leapt to her feet in fright. Everything was awake. Horses were rearing up on their hind legs and snorting in terror. She grabbed a horse's mane and jumped on his back.

In an instant the herd was galloping away like the wind. She called to the horses to stop, but her voice was lost in the thunder. Nothing could stop them. She hugged her horse's neck with her fingers twisted into his mane. She clung on, afraid of falling under the drumming hooves.

The horses galloped faster and faster, pursued by the thunder and lightning. They swept like a brown flood across hills and through valleys. Fear drove them on and on, leaving their familiar grazing grounds far behind.

At last the storm disappeared over the horizon. The tired horses slowed and then stopped and rested. Stars came out and the moon shone over hills the girl had never seen before. She knew they were lost.

Next morning she was wakened by a loud neighing. A beautiful spotted stallion was prancing to and fro in front of her, stamping his hooves and shaking his mane. He was strong and proud and more handsome than any horse she had ever dreamed of. He told her that he was the leader of all the wild horses who roamed the hills. He welcomed her to live with them. She was glad, and all her horses lifted their heads and neighed joyfully, happy to be free with the wild horses.

The people searched everywhere for the girl and the vanished horses. They were nowhere to be found.

But a year later two hunters rode into the hills where the wild horses lived. When they climbed a hill and looked over the top they saw the wild horses led by the beautiful spotted stallion. Beside him rode the girl leading a colt. They called out to her. She waved back, but the stallion quickly drove her away with all his horses.

The hunters galloped home and told what they had seen. The men mounted their fastest horses and set out at once.

It was a long chase. The stallion defended the girl and the colt. He circled round and round them so that the riders could not get near. They tried to catch him with ropes but he dodged them. He had no fear. His eyes shone like cold stars. He snorted and his hooves struck as fast as lightning.

The riders admired his courage. They might never have caught the girl except her horse stumbled and she fell.

She was glad to see her parents and they thought she would be happy to be home again. But they soon saw she was sad and missed the colt and the wild horses.

Each evening as the sun went down people would hear the stallion neighing sadly from the hilltop above the village, calling for her to come back.

The days passed. Her parents knew the girl was lonely. She became ill and the doctors could do nothing to help her. They asked what would make her well again. "I love to run with the wild horses," she answered. "They are my relatives. If you let me go back to them I shall be happy for evermore."

Her parents loved her and agreed that she should go back to live with the wild horses. They gave her a beautiful dress and the best horse in the village to ride.

The spotted stallion led his wild horses down from the hills. The people gave them fine things to wear: colorful blankets and decorated saddles. They painted designs on their bodies and tied eagle feathers and ribbons in their manes and tails.

In return, the girl gave the colt to her parents. Everyone was joyful.

Once again the girl rode beside the spotted stallion. They were proud and happy together.

But she did not forget her people. Each year she would come back, and she always brought her parents a colt.

And then one year she did not return and was never seen again. But when hunters next saw the wild horses there galloped beside the mighty stallion a beautiful mare with a mane and tail floating like wispy clouds about her. They said the girl had surely become one of the wild horses at last.

Today we are still glad to remember that we have relatives among the Horse People. And it gives us joy to see the wild horses running free. Our thoughts fly with them.